Lucy's family launches into the cyber-world!

Nina Du Thaler

Hi, my name is Elle.

I'm just an ordinary kid. I'm not sure what I'm going to be when I grow up but I'm sure I'm destined for greatness.

I always wonder about growing up. I wish I could grow up faster. Whenever I ask a grown-up if I can do something new, they give me a strange look and say, "Don't wish your childhood away!" or "Maybe when you're a little older." I wonder when that day will come because I am older each day than I was the day before!

What's interesting about me? Hmmm, let me think...

When I was little I found my name very confusing. First, I learned about the letters of the alphabet and for a long time I thought my name was spelled "L". Then, I learned it was actually "E" "L" "L" "E". Very weird! It has sort of stuck now and I sign cards and letters "L".

I've made a shocking discovery that I don't know much about cyber-safety. In fact, I don't even know what cyber-safety means. How embarrassing!

I'm sharing my diary and what I've learned with you to save you this embarrassment.

Cyber-safety is all about how to safely use the Internet, computers, mobile phones, tablets and other cool gadgets.

I also have a totally cool group of friends who are going to help us with this. Together, we will explore the cyber-world so you don't have to make any of our mistakes.

Let me introduce my friends …

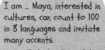

I am ... Lizzy, always happy and singing and try to see the bright side of things

I Think ... Elle is my BFF (Best Friend Forever)

I am ... Maya, interested in cultures, can count to 100 in 8 languages and imitate many accents

I Think ... I want to be a librarian

I am ... Tom, very popular, have the latest fashion and can do any sports really well

I Think...... I have all cool gadgets there are

I am ... Lucy, a tiny girl with a huge brain and can solve any math problem

I Think. ... I love numbers more than anything

I am ... Dennis, a bit nerdy but really cool inside and can remember everything ever said to me

I Think ... I can beat Tom running one day

I am ... Elle, an ordinary kid, willing to learn and destined for greatness

I Think ... I have the best friends ever

Wednesday

Maths class – ugh! Mathlete Competition announcement!

Tick-tock, tick-tock. Mrs Hudson was going on and on about maths – equations, numbers, fractions. Jibber, jabber … jibber, jabber. And all I could hear was the ticking of the classroom clock up on the wall. I had almost drifted into a daydream about sand and rolling waves, which is something I do a lot, when I felt a jab in my right upper arm.

Gasp! I almost cried out in surprise, then looked over to see Lizzy, my absolute best friend forever (BFF), giving me a panicked, wide-eyed look. "Elle," she leaned over to whisper, "Mrs Hudson asked you a question." My gaze went from Lizzy's green eyes up to my favourite teacher who was looking directly at me. Whoops!

Mrs Hudson wore her dark brown, almost black hair in a tight bun on the top of her head, like a ballerina. She also wore a disappointed smile as she looked at me. I love, love, love my teacher, which is why I would hate to let her down.

"Sorry, Mrs Hudson," I said as I quickly sat up straighter. "What was that?"

Her eyes softened a little and she said, "I was just asking if you could read your answer for problem 14 from last night's homework. The fraction word problem?"

Gulp! The mere mention of fractions made it feel like there was a lump in my throat and my heartbeat went faster and faster – thump, thump – in my chest! I might love Mrs Hudson, but I most definitely did not love maths. All those numbers and symbols and complicated word problems made my head spin around – it made me dizzy!

Luckily, I'd answered all twenty questions from the homework, but I was pretty sure they weren't all correct. I pulled the worksheet out and cleared my throat before reading my answer. "Uh, I think it's one-third?"

Mrs Hudson smiled kindly. "Hmm, good try, Elle, but I'm afraid it's not quite right. Lizzy?"

I looked at Lizzy who blushed and answered, "I got one-eighth."

Mrs Hudson nodded. "That's right, very good,

Lizzy." And then she went on and on while my mind went round and round.

Lizzy shot me a look that said, 'Sorry – what could I do?' and I gave her a weak smile in return.

At the end of class, Mrs Hudson made an announcement. "There's going to be a maths competition on Friday of next week and students from any grade are welcome to sign up. Each school in the region will send a team of three top-level mathletes to the competition. If anyone's interested, come see me about signing up!"

A maths competition?! I didn't even know there was such a thing ... Was it like my very sporty friend Tom's race competition that I'd helped him train for and ran in myself? How strange! And definitely not for me – no way. Yikes!

But my mind drifted to the image of my friend Lucy with her thick-rimmed glasses. She was a serious maths whiz and had been put in the year ahead of us even though she was ten just like me. She would be sooo perfect for it!

Classes went on and on: some fun and some not so much fun. Then lunch and then they went on some more until – briiiing! The final bell for the school day sounded and I rushed down the hallway towards the doors that led outside when wham! I ran straight into a very out-of-breath Lucy. Her face was pink and she pushed her black hair behind an ear as she grabbed my arm in excitement.

"Elle, guess what?!" she asked as we both walked out the doors into the bright sunshine.

"What?" I asked with an equally excited smile, though I had a feeling I knew what she was going to say.

"I just signed up for the maths competition Friday next week!"

Yup, I'd guessed right! But I pretended to be surprised and grinned at her as I said, "Really? Lucy that's sooo cool! You're going to get on the team for sure!"

Lucy gave a little skip on the path. "I hope so," she said as she pushed her big glasses further up her delicate nose. "There's only three people for each school. They'll decide who made the team this Friday – day after tomorrow."

I gave Lucy's arm a reassuring squeeze. "I'm

absolutely, one hundred per cent positive you'll make it. No-one at school's as good as you with numbers, not even the older kids!"

And when she did make the team, maybe I could help her study. I could use some maths practice myself …

Friday

Lucy makes the team! Operation: help Lucy train!

Thursday went by in a whirr – school, eating, sleeping and a bit of homework. Then Friday arrived, and everyone was talking at lunch about who was going to make the maths competition team. Finally the last class was over and I was about to run down the hall to where all of my friends and I planned to meet Lucy.

Except I saw a teacher for an older grade watching, and we're not supposed to run in the halls, so I speed-walked as fast as possible out the doors to join Lucy and the group. They treat us like such babies sometimes – honestly!

Lucy was beaming as brightly as the sun outside. "I made it! And I'm the only one in my grade to make the team, the other two students are a year above me!"

I jumped up and down and gave her a big hug while our friend Maya said, "That's amazing, Lucy!" Maya used her impression of a Russian accent, which was her current favourite. She love,

love, loved accents from all over the world and had a new one just about every week.

"It's sooo awesome," I gushed. "Can I help you train, or whatever it is you do to get ready for a maths competition?"

Our friend Tom, who is super strong and good at sports, spoke before Lucy could. "A maths competition?" he asked. "That's cool, but what do you do exactly? Is it like the Twilight Run I competed in?" Tom had gotten first place in his age category in that run. He's crazy fast!

Lucy tilted her head and put a finger to her chin to think. Then she said, "Hmmm. I guess it's kind of like your Twilight Run, Tom, since there's going to be prizes for first and second place, and it's a competition too. But instead of running, we'll answer maths problems as a team. Stuff like fractions, statistic word problems, geometric equations …"

Blah … blah … blah – she went on and on listing tons of complicated-sounding maths terms, so many that my head started to spin. Whoa!

Then Lucy looked at me and said, "And you can totally help me with the practice questions, Elle, if you want. My maths teacher helped the team members download a cool, safe and secure computer program that has sample questions on the competition maths level!"

"Yay – definitely!" I said with a smile. This could help improve my own maths skills. Woo hoo!

Lizzy spoke up. "Oh, that's good, Lucy. My dad warned me about only downloading computer programs that you know are from trusted sites, like the ones that have a tick symbol or check mark for safety."

I bobbed my head up and down and added, "Exactly! And if you're not sure, ask someone you trust, like your maths teacher." I was excited to share my ever-growing cyber-safety knowledge!

We all chatted a little more, then Lucy and I walked to the bus stop so we could ride home together. She whistled and skipped every now and then, so excited that she'd made the team. After we got on the bus and found a seat to share, Lucy's mobile phone made a buzzzz sound and she took it out of her backpack.

"It's a text from my mum," she told me and then she read it out loud.

We have two
new 'family
members' at
home today –
it's a
surprise!
See u soon
xxoo – Mum

Lucy's eyebrows came together in confusion. "New family members?" she wondered aloud. "Did we get new pets to keep Lolita company?" Lolita was Lucy's family pet parrot. She liked to talk – a lot!

I shrugged my shoulders and smiled. "Will you text me when you find out what they are?!" I asked.

"Definitely," she said. "And, Elle … do you want to come help me do practice questions tomorrow at my house?"

"Absolutely." I nodded eagerly. "I want you to win for our school." Then I thought for a moment and said, "Not that winning is the important part

– it's about giving it a go and having fun!"

We talked more as we rode the bus and, after I had a super special snack of freshly baked chocolate chip cookies at home, I went up to my room to work on homework.

Homework was like a box of chocolates: some 'flavours' I liked a lot and some of them just weren't my favourite 'taste'. Today it was mostly boring … boring … and more boring – ugh!

I need some music to make this more fun, I thought to myself. So I got out my mobile phone, put on a très cool new song and began to sing along with it. I really, really loved to sing, though I wasn't sure other people would even call it singing.

I had left my homework on my desk and got up to do some awesome dance moves along with the music when, beeep! My phone sounded with a text alert. I jumped in the middle of my spinning dance move and put a hand over my heart. Eek – that had startled me! I grabbed my phone and saw it was a text from Lucy.

Ooh! My family had a regular computer at home too, but we didn't have a tablet. Note to self – ask Mum if we can get a tablet as well!

Saturday

Helping Lucy! Tablets, computers and grumpy older brother!

Pop! It was Saturday morning, which meant swimming with my BFF Lizzy, and then going to Lucy's house to help with her maths practice. I shot out of my bed like a piece of popcorn on a hot pan!

Some days I liked to really take my time to wake up, especially when it wasn't a school day. But today I was excited to head to swimming and then Lucy's where I could meet their new 'family members'.

At swimming, we did these friendly-type races amongst ourselves. It was our own mini competition!

After coming in second for the freestyle stroke, I grabbed my towel and sat on a plastic chair near the pool to dry off and catch my breath. Lizzy came and sat next to me, her usual super happy and smiling face beaming at me as she wrung her long blond hair out with her towel.

"So," she said, "you said Lucy's family got a tablet and a computer for the family? I'm sooo jealous!"

She laughed and I nodded while trying to get the water out of my left ear. Whack … whack. I gently hit the other side of my head to clear my waterlogged ear.

"I know," I told her. "I'm totally jealous too. Do you think I should ask my parents for a tablet?"

Lizzy shrugged and grinned. "Doesn't hurt to ask, right?" she said.

I completely agreed. We got to talking about Lucy, and the new tablet and computer.

"You know," Lizzy said, "it is really important to be careful what kind of personal information and photos or even comments you put out there into the cyber-world. My dad told me that anything you put out there on the Internet stays there forever. And nasty people could see and use it, so we should be super, super careful!"

I listened to my BFF, making mental notes to put this into my diary later.

After going home for some lunch and a little relaxing, my mum drove me over to Lucy's house.

"Nice to see you, Elle." Lucy's mum smiled at me as I came in the front door.

"You too." I smiled back and waved at Lucy's mum. She was thin and pale just like Lucy, except she didn't wear glasses.

Lucy came up and gave an excited little jump. "Hey, Elle, thanks for coming over!" she said.

Suddenly there was a loud squawk! It came from behind and made me jump and turn around. I laughed.

"Oh, hi, Lolita, I didn't see you there," I told their pet parrot who swung on a perch in a large golden cage on a table. Her bright red, blue, yellow and green feathers looked like a cheery rainbow. I wished we had a parrot!

"See you there … squawk … Lolita see you there." She repeated part of my sentence like she usually did. Everyone laughed and Lolita excitedly shuffled her sharp, pointy feet. (Do parrots have feet or talons … or is it claws?! I made a mental note to research that later.)

Then Lucy turned to her mum. "Can we use the tablet so Elle and I can practise questions on that app from my teacher?"

Just then Lucy's older brother, Kevin, who had just turned fourteen and thought that meant he was pretty much an adult, came down the stairs. "Wait a minute," he said as his dark eyebrows pulled into a frown, "I wanted to use the tablet to play the new 'Elden Wizard' online game with my friends. It's a free multi-player game and …"

Lucy's mum held up a finger and cut in. "Now hold on, Kevin, remember what we told you two." She looked between Kevin and Lucy with a serious expression. "You have to be careful what sites you go to and what apps you install or download. Especially if this online game is free, you have to be careful about using it and putting in any personal information like your full name and address. It could put your privacy at risk."

Lucy nodded eagerly, and gave her brother a smug look before saying, "I remember, Mum. And the program I want to download and install is super safe since it's approved by our school. Plus it has that little lock symbol my maths teacher showed me that means all the private information is secure."

Her mum beamed proudly at Lucy and I noticed

Kevin crossing his arms over his chest and narrowing his eyes at his sister. He didn't look at all happy.

"That's very good," her mum said, then turned to Kevin. "Lucy can use the tablet because it's for an academic competition and it sounds like the app is safe to install. Maybe you can use it after Lucy's practice, that is after your dad and I check out this free Elden Warlocks game." She smiled then turned to go into the kitchen and we followed.

"It's Elden Wizards, not Warlocks," I heard Kevin mumble as we followed their mum out of the room. He looked very, very grumpy.

Then Lolita called out, "Elden Wizards … Elden Wizards!" and Kevin stomped back off upstairs.

Lucy, her mum and I walked into their big kitchen, which had a long table with benches on either side of it. Her dad was sitting at the table facing us, but focused on the new computer in front of him while he sipped some tea. Lucy's dad absolutely loooved herbal tea and biscuits.

"Honey, you're back from work already!" Then Lucy's mum frowned at her husband. "Should we really have the computer in here with all the food?

You might spill tea on the keyboard or get biscuit crumbs in between the keys."

"True, but I'll be careful," her dad replied, then glanced at Lucy and me. "Hi, Elle; hey, Lulu." He used his usual nickname for Lucy, which I thought was pretty cute. But only her dad called her Lulu.

"Hi," Lucy and I chorused in response. Her mum opened the fridge and looked at us. "You two want some study snacks?" We both nodded eagerly and in two minutes had apples, chips and peppermint stick candies. Yum!

"We're going to practise up in my room," Lucy said as we carried the food and the tablet towards the kitchen door.

"Okay," her mum answered. "Just remember to stick with that teacher-approved practice question app. I installed some Internet-filtering software on the tablet this morning. That will help block unwanted or nasty content just in case."

Lucy gave a thumbs-up and I filed away this 'filtering software' term in my brain to write in my diary later. There was sooo much to learn about cyber-safety and I wanted to make sure I wrote it all down.

Lucy and I had finished the apples, half a bag of chips and one peppermint stick each ten minutes later. Now I was sprawled out on my stomach across Lucy's bedroom beanbag chair. Lucy sat cross-legged on a low, cushy chair facing me, the tablet in her hands.

It was so cool that she could just hold it like that, the tablet being so lightweight – unlike a laptop or desktop computer. I wanted one now more than ever!

"Oh look," Lucy suddenly declared, staring at the tablet's screen. "The practice question app is fully downloaded and installed. Ready to start?" She looked at me with a grin and held out the tablet.

"Yes," I said as I greedily snatched the tablet from her hands, a thrill running through my veins. Finally, I was holding the much-desired tablet.

Lucy eyed me warily. "Just be super, duper careful not to drop it, or accidentally click on some weird pop-up ad or something. You never know if a site is really what they say it is. Dad told me all about phishing for information."

Huh? My nose scrunched up in puzzlement. "Fishing? Like we did on that school camping trip last year at the lake? You know when Maya caught that squirmy little blue fish?"

Lucy laughed and pushed her glasses up on her nose while shaking her head. "No, not that kind of fishing," she explained. "It starts with a 'ph' not an 'f' and it's when others try to get personal information from you, through the online world. Like if you click on links you don't know or answer emails from someone you don't know."

Wow! It seemed like Lucy knew a ton more about cyber-safety than me. This was yet another one to remember and write in my diary later. Whew, there was a lot to remember today!

"Okay, got it," I told her with a nod of my head. "No clicking on weird links accidentally. And … ooh. It's so cool that tablets have touch screens!" I interrupted myself as I touched the round image next to practice question number one.

"I know, sooo cool, right?" Lucy's dark brown eyes glimmered. "Okay, I have some paper and my calculator. I'm ready for the first question. And the program should time how long it takes me to answer the questions." She sat up straighter and adjusted the notepad on her lap.

My eyebrows rose up. "You get to use a calculator?" I asked.

"Yup," Lucy answered. "It's all about coming up with the correct answer in a certain amount of time that each team is allowed. I'm actually going to be practising with the two other team members on Monday, but I want to be sure I'm super prepared. I saw them in school Friday and they look sooo big. The girl's clothes are so grown-up and sophisticated. So let's go!"

"Okay." I looked down at the first practice question and read: "If you roll two six-sided die, what are the chances that your total will be 6? Express your answer as a ratio using the colon (:) sign." Eek! I had no idea how to find the answer to this one. Just reading it made my head go into a whirlwind!

But Lucy wasn't fazed one bit. She got right to work with her pencil, notepad and calculator. She was sooo going to show those older, bigger students how awesome she was and rock the competition next Friday!

Sunday

Outdoor maths training, and ice-cream!

This afternoon, Dad dropped me off at a nearby park to meet Lucy – so we could do more practice questions. Lucy's mum and dad thought it would be a good idea for her to get some fresh air while she trained.

It was a nice day with part sun and part puffy white clouds that looked like big cotton balls and made me wish I was floating away on one like it was a pillow!

We were sitting on a bench and had just finished a round of geometry-related word problems (yikes!) when Lucy pulled out a bag full of celery sticks and then one with peanut butter cookies. Celery made my stomach twist and my nose squish up – blech! But the cookies were delicious. Yummm!

After we ate Lucy said, "Guess what happened this morning?"

I swallowed my last bite of cookie. "What?" I asked. "Did you get more cool gadgets at your house?"

She shook her head and crunched down on a celery stick. Crunch-munch ... munch-crunch.

"Nope," she said. "My dad spilled coffee on the computer and Mum got really mad and said, 'I told you so'." Lucy's eyes were wide as she went on. "Luckily, it didn't ruin the computer or keyboard or anything, and we cleaned it up quickly. But now it's at a desk in the living room with a new 'no food or drink rule!' Mum says it's better for your posture and eyesight anyway to have it at a proper desk with good lighting."

Then she thought for a moment and added, "Mum said she found out it's really not good to even have the tablet in my bedroom. She said I can, but only if I sit at my desk and make sure there's good light in the room. Otherwise my eyesight could get even worse. I don't want bigger glasses than these!" She lifted her thick-framed glasses up and down, and we laughed.

"So," I said after considering this, "are those big, dark grey clouds going to be bad for us looking at the tablet?" I pointed up at the gathering storm clouds that brewed overhead. They had chased away the puffy white clouds while we worked.

Lucy looked up too. "Should be okay," she said.

"But I guess we should go soon. Dad actually said to make sure I get plenty of physical exercise and don't just spend all my time on the computer or tablet. If you don't do active stuff with your body then you might have trouble sleeping and you also might become less healthy."

I gave a half-smile and pulled a Frisbee out of the backpack I'd brought. "That's funny," I said. "My dad said the same thing and made me bring this so we could exercise our bodies and not just our brains. He said it actually makes your mind sharper when you do physical activity. It'll help you win the competition!"

So, we did four more questions, some involving the dreaded fraction problems – shiver – then packed up our snack wrappers and threw the Frisbee around in the grassy field near the bench for a bit.

Then – rumble, rumble … boom … crack! "Aahh!" we both screamed out as the thunder sounded from above and the sky blinked with lightning. The thunder echoed through the park and I could feel it in my skin. Major goosebumps!

"Quick!" I grabbed Lucy's arm with one hand and the Frisbee and my satchel in the other. "We better get out of here before it starts to … " But I was too late. Pitter-patter … patter-pitter! The rain was coming down on our heads.

"Oh no, the tablet!" Lucy cried, then put it safely in her backpack. "Whew," she said. "That was close. Water could really damage it!" Then the rain came down harder.

"Eek!" Lucy squealed as I cried out, "Yikes!" We then really got our exercise as we sprinted to the edge of the park where our parents were supposed to pick us up soon. My heart was beating so hard my lungs hurt, but we were giggling and laughing as we stood on the grass.

"Oh, look," Lucy said between giggles as our hair dripped with the rain, "your dad and my mum are here. Thank goodness!" She pointed to the two cars parked at the curb in front of us.

I ran up to my dad's car as Lucy ran to hers. I called out, "Thank goodness is right! See you Monday, Lucy. And thanks!"

She waved and got into her car as I waved and got into mine. "Bye! See you Monday!" she called back.

I was a soggy mess when I got into the seat and turned to look at Dad. It was like I'd been swimming again, except this time I hadn't gotten wet on purpose.

"Whoa, I should've brought a towel," Dad said with both of his eyebrows raised and a grin on his face.

"I know." I grinned back, wiping water out of my eyes.

"You know," my dad said as he drove down the road, "I was going to take you to get ice-cream, but now … " Wait, what? Ice-cream?! Hold on …

"Don't worry." Dad laughed as he took in my worried expression. "We can still go; let's just stop by home so you can dry off and change first." Oh, okay – whew!

The rain, thunder and lightning chased us all the way home. After I'd changed into my très cool – and très dry – jeans and a cute yellow top, we headed to the ice-cream shop.

"One triple chocolate fudge in a cone please," I chirped to the ice-cream guy. Two minutes later Dad and I sat at a round table inside the ice-cream shop. I was in chocolate heaven as I ate the creamy, sweet, cold goodness – mmmm!

Bing! A sudden idea popped into my head as I looked up at my dad eating his mint chocolate chip ice-cream in a sugar cone. I hadn't asked Mum about getting a tablet yet, and since Dad was more easily persuaded, not to mention softened up by eating such a yummy treat, it seemed like the perfect opportunity.

"So, Dad," I began in what I hoped was a casual, cool voice, "did I tell you how Lucy's family got a computer and a tablet?"

He was mid-bite with his cone and gave a muffled grunt as an answer. I took that as my cue to continue.

"And, as you know, I've been helping her train for the maths competition this Friday. It was so awesome and so easy to take the tablet to the park today. We got fresh air while also doing practice maths problems."

This was all leading up to the big question. He chewed slower and looked at me with slightly curious, or perhaps they were suspicious, eyes. Now for the final part in the logical build-up.

"So, since I'm not a maths genius like Lucy, and there's so many safe and secure maths learning programs out there, I thought that it would be great for my academic development if we could also get a tablet – for all of us to use."

Silence. That was all that followed my little speech for what felt like forever.

Dad finished up his cone, wiped his fingers with a napkin and then looked at me with a thoughtful frown. "Hmm, well, sweetheart," he finally said, "maybe when you're older."

Ugh – nooo! Not the dreaded 'when you're older' answer! I heard that all the time, but now that I was ten, double digits, I thought I was indeed 'older' at this point! But apparently not.

Then, before I could come up with an argument, he went on, "Besides, you have to be extra careful with tablets, especially if you want to take them to someplace where you're not using the home Wi-Fi network – like overseas, or the park or school. In those places, the tablet has to use 4G connectivity to the Internet and it costs much, much more. We can't afford a huge bill for that."

Whoa, he was really getting worked up about this.

My shoulders went down a bit in defeat, but at least I had my ice-cream as well as more cyber-world facts to write down.

Monday and Tuesday

Weird dream …

Monday morning I caught the school bus and breathed in a nice, cool gust of air that came through the open window next to my seat. The dewy morning air really helped me wake up, especially on a Monday. Sniff … sniff … sniiiiffff! Aah!

When the bus stopped to pick up more kids, my friend Dennis got on and sat next to me. Dennis wore tortoiseshell-rimmed glasses and was super tall and skinny, just like a beanstalk. This always seemed strange to me because the boy ate and ate all the time, yet still declared he was hungry. Crazy!

Even now as he sat next to me, Dennis was eating a breakfast bar with oats and chocolate chips – mmm, melt-in-your-mouth chocolate chips. Crunch … crunch … munch. "Morning, Elle," he said through his mouthful. "Want one of these?" He pulled another bar from his backpack, but I held up a hand.

"That's okay, thanks." We chatted about this and

that, then I brought up my new favourite subject: Lucy's family tablet and how I was helping her train for this Friday. I mentioned how Lucy told me she was going to bring the tablet to school this week.

"You know," Dennis said, now sipping from a chocolate milk box, "I hope Lucy put a really, really strong password on it, one that she didn't write down like I did." And here Dennis, who tells the most detailed, descriptive stories of anyone I know, launched into a tale I knew firsthand, but I listened anyway.

Basically, Dennis had written his password down on a piece of paper and lost it at school one day. The bad thing was he'd used the same exact password for all of his online accounts, so someone might have found it, snuck in and saw all his private information, texts and photos! Luckily our friend Maya found it and all was okay. But we'd learned a valuable lesson from his experience!

At lunch that day, I made sure to tell Lucy what Dennis had said about passwords and she changed hers to something even stronger. Go me! I'm a cyber-safety superhero. Woo hoo!

Sometimes I have the strangest dreams ever, and Tuesday morning I found myself in one of the oddest dreams yet.

I was at one of my most fav … fav … favourite places in the world: sand warm and crunchy under my bare feet, sunglasses on to shield my eyes from the glorious bright sunshine and the smell of refreshing salt water. Yup, I was at the beach!

Swish, swoosh … crash! The ocean waves came rolling and crashing over and over not five metres from where I sat in the sand. Then I shifted my sunglasses to sit on top of my head and looked out at the blue-green ocean water, sparkling in the sun.

As I walked towards the water and let the lovely, cool water wash over my hot feet, I noticed something really weird out in the water. I stepped further and squinted my eyes for a better look. There were dark-coloured numbers and maths symbols floating around like buoys. Whoa – very strange!

Suddenly dark grey clouds rolled in and blocked out the sunlight. Rumble … crack … boom! The air around me shook and made the hairs on the back of my neck stand up. Yikes!

Next thing I knew, I was staring outside from my bedroom window where I could see dark clouds along with raindrops.

Blink … blink, rub … rub. I tried to get the sleepiness out of my eyes and also make my racing heart slow down. That dream had been a bit scary! And what had it meant?

Probably just because there's an actual storm outside, plus all that maths competition training with Lucy, I told myself.

Still, I wanted to make sure Lucy was okay, so I went over to the big kids' side of school at lunchtime. She seemed just as happy and fine as ever. Actually she was proud of a new document she'd been working on, compiling notes, tips and answers for practice maths questions.

"I'm going to show it to the other two team members when we meet today after school." She grinned proudly as she held up the tablet where she'd typed the document. She went on, "I just showed it to my maths teacher, who was very impressed, but she told me to make sure I save the file as I go and also to make certain there's a backup copy just in case. But I have to grab lunch and it's only a backup – I still have the original – so I'll just do it later."

My forehead wrinkled up in a frown. "Are you sure? You don't want to lose it after all that work," I said, my mind flashing to the dream of maths symbols on the ocean and the scary thunderstorm.

But Lucy gave a quirky half-smile and shook her head. "I won't," she said confidently. "The only way I'd lose it is if some kind of virus got into the tablet and made it crash or something like that. Besides, I'll do it later anyway. Gotta run – byeee!" And she was off before I could say anything else.

Virus? Like when I had that horrible, stuffy-nosed cold two weeks ago? I'd have to ask her about that later.

After school that day, while I was doing some fun homework for geography – all about beaches around the world – my phone pinged with a new email. It was from Lucy.

```
Hey L - Just finished the meeting
with the other maths competition team
members and they seem sooo much older
and kind of … different. One of them
is always fidgeting with his shirt
```

collar, which he has buttoned all the
way up. And the girl acts like a
know-it-all, even though I could
answer three practice questions they
got incorrect answers for - ha! I
like practising with you better!:)
Can we train more tomorrow?

I grinned and wrote back right away.

Of course - I'll ask my mum and dad
if I can ride home with you on the
bus tomorrow! And that's sooo cool
you got those three questions right
and beat those older team members -
woo hoo! :) L

Wednesday

Video games and viruses!!

Pitter-patter … patter-pitter. Today was another rainy, cloudy, stormy day – yuck. But I was still excited to be heading over to Lucy's house to help her one last time before Friday's maths meet. She had more mathlete team practice tomorrow after school.

I rode the bus home with Lucy. As soon as we walked into her house, I gave their parrot Lolita's feathery head a little scratch-scratch through the cage bars, which she loooved. Then Lucy and I went into the kitchen for snacks.

As we left the living room, Lolita called out, "Shh … secret … it's a secret – squawk!"

Lucy and I looked at each other with curious frowns, then burst into giggles. "Ooh, I think Lolita has a secret," I sing-songed teasingly. We both stopped short when we saw Kevin sitting at the kitchen table scoffing down a ham sandwich and chips.

He paused mid-bite and looked at us, his dark eyes wide. I couldn't be sure, but he seemed a little nervous for some reason. Huh ... weird. Then he shot up from the table and rushed to the pantry.

"You guys want some snacks to help you train?" he asked glancing at me and Lucy as he grabbed corn chips, savoury biscuits, jelly beans and drinks to hand to us. Lucy and I exchanged puzzled looks. Her older brother was acting extremely odd. He'd never abandoned his own food to offer his little sister and friend stuff before. Hmm ...

Lucy just shrugged and said, "Uh ... okaaaay. Thanks, Kevin." We took the snacks and left Kevin in the kitchen with an overly cheery smile on his face.

After properly charging our bodies and minds with food, Lucy and I both sat at wooden chairs at her bedroom desk – to make sure our postures were nice and straight – and turned on the bright desk light so we wouldn't strain our eyes.

I slid my fingers over the tablet to get to the fraction word-problem section of the practice questions, like Lucy had asked, and gave a small shudder. I had another fractions homework sheet due tomorrow. Maybe this would help me understand those a bit better.

But, when I tapped the round image next to the first question, something really, really strange happened. Well, actually to be more precise, nothing happened. And then a smaller rectangular box popped up in middle of the tablet's screen. It blinked in and out and read:

```
Warning! Your Device Has Been
Infected With A Virus!!
```

I gasped and turned the tablet to show Lucy. "Oh no, Lucy, look! It's that virus thing you were talking about the other day!" Lucy snatched the tablet from my hands and gaped as she looked down at the blinking message. Her pale face turned bright, strawberry-red and then a pale greenish colour. Was she going to be sick?!

"Oh no, no, no! This can't be happening!" she cried, quickly tapping on the message, which also had an 'okay – get help' button. "I might lose the practice question app and …" She looked up at me with wide, watery eyes that started to fog up her glasses lenses. "Elle, I didn't back up those notes like my maths teacher told me. I got so busy, then I forgot!"

My eyes flew from her to the screen, which now seemed to be shutting down all the programs, and then it suddenly turned off. The tablet screen had gone black and lifeless! "Um, maybe we should check with your parents and they can help get rid of the virus and get your files back?"

Lucy nodded, wiping at a tear underneath her glasses. "Mum's at work, but I think Dad's here," she said with a bit of hope in her voice. We raced downstairs with the tablet and found Kevin now in the living room watching some fantasy TV series from the couch. He loooved anything to do with fantasy – like elves, wizards, dragons and stuff – or sci-fi (science fiction) with intergalactic battles and spaceships.

"Kevin, where's Dad?" Lucy asked in a high-pitched voice. Kevin looked from the TV to his sister and then to the tablet in her hands.

"Dad's just out shopping; he'll be back soon. So, I'm the grown-up in the house now," he declared proudly, then asked, "What do you need Dad for – what's wrong?"

Before Lucy could answer I blurted out, "The tablet just got sick … I mean got a virus and Lucy tapped 'okay' to a virus warning thingy that was all blinky and now it's dead … I mean it's shut down!" Both Kevin and Lucy stared at me for a second, then Lucy nodded and more tears streamed out.

"I didn't save my notes! What if they're gone forever?" she asked.

Kevin, to my surprise, answered encouragingly. "It's okay, Lucy, even if they're gone you're like a major maths genius and you have all that knowledge locked up here." He tapped his head.

Lucy looked a little less anxious. Good, maybe this whole thing would be okay. And Kevin was right; she knew all of this stuff backwards and forwards. She didn't need those notes or that practice question app, not really.

Then Lolita piped up, "Elden Wizards ... squawk ... Elden Wizards! Shh ... secret ... it's a secret!" Whoosh! All three of our heads quickly swivelled towards the brightly coloured bird.

Huh? Wasn't that the name of the free online game Kevin had been grumpy about before? I was still trying to wrap my head around it when Lucy's face turned so red it almost looked purple and her eyes got all narrow and squinty as she glared at her brother.

"Kevin," she said in a low, angry tone, "you didn't have anything to do with this, did you? Why is Lolita talking about secrets and that Elden Wizards game you wanted so badly but Mum and Dad said wasn't secure enough?"

Kevin shot Lolita a dirty look then crossed his arms. "Fine. Last night when everyone was upstairs, I snuck the tablet and downloaded Elden Wizards. Happy now?"

Lucy stepped closer to her brother. I could practically see steaming-hot smoke coming out of her ears! Yikes – this wasn't going to be pretty. Lucy was usually so cool, calm and collected. I'd never seen her this angry before.

"Happy?!" she shouted. "You just let a virus attack my … I mean our family's new tablet! And now my notes – that I didn't back up – and maybe the progress recorded in the practice maths question app are all gone because of your stupid, kid wizard game!!"

All I could do was watch, standing between Kevin, who was now standing to my left near the couch, and Lucy who stood to my right. As I looked from one to the other, it felt like watching a very angry tennis match.

Kevin now shot back with: "Well you should've backed up your work! Everyone knows to do that! And maybe it was all your fault clicking 'okay' on that virus warning! Since you're so smart, you should know people out there make fake virus alerts to trick you. I bet that's what let the virus in!"

Wow, boys could be so, so, sooo mean, especially older brothers. And people could be mean too! Who would trick innocent people and into letting in this virus thingy into their devices? How horribly awful!

I turned back to look at Lucy as Lolita repeated, "Virus in … let the virus in … squawk!" Ugh, Lolita was definitely not helping right now. Lucy looked like she wasn't sure if she should cry or be even madder.

Finally, she opened her mouth and yelled back, "I can't believe you're blaming me when you were the one to disobey Mum and Dad to get that game. All I did was try to fix it and …"

Kevin interrupted her, making my head swish back to look at him. "You should've waited for Dad to come home and told him about it before clicking that link!" Just as he yelled this, the front door opened and closed shut. Slam!

Lucy's dad put down two paper bags of groceries and furrowed his brow at Lucy and Kevin. "Waited to tell me what? And what link?"

I gulped so hard it hurt my throat. I almost wanted to slink away from all of this drama, but of course I had to stay to support Lucy – and to see what happened!

Twenty minutes later, after Kevin, Lucy and I explained what had happened to the tablet, and Kevin got computer privileges taken away for the week for not listening, we all sat in the living room more calmly.

Now Lucy's dad held the tablet and told us he'd tried to put it in safe mode and deleted the Elden Wizards game, but that hadn't worked.

"So now," he told us while adjusting his round-rimmed glasses, "we have to do what's called a factory reset to get rid of the virus and then I don't want either of you downloading or installing anything else on this – just to be sure, okay?" Both of them nodded sadly and he looked at Lucy.

"Sweetheart, I know you didn't mean to," he said

gently, "but when you tapped 'okay' on that virus warning, that's what let the virus in, not Kevin's online game. So next time just wait until Mum or I can look at it or ask a trusted person like your maths teacher for help, okay?"

Lucy nodded weakly, looking like she might cry. Kevin looked just the tiniest bit triumphant. He'd been right about how the virus got in.

Maybe getting these two new 'family members' was causing more turmoil in Lucy's household than fun …

Friday

Day of the maths competition!!

Today started off all icky and rainy again. Ugh, where was the sun?! I looked through all the clothes in my closet twice, not finding anything very thrilling to wear until I spotted something bright yellow. It was one of my comfy school dresses.

I put it on and smiled at myself in the mirror. Even if the sky decided to stay grey and cloudy, at least I could add a little sunshine with my très cool outfit!

I hadn't seen Lucy all day yesterday, not even a glimpse in the hallway on the big kids' side of school. So today at lunch, after nearly inhaling my tomato and cheese sandwich, two carrot sticks and a few gulps of water, I texted Lucy.

It was almost the end of lunchtime and I was about to go look for her when my mobile buzzed with her reply.

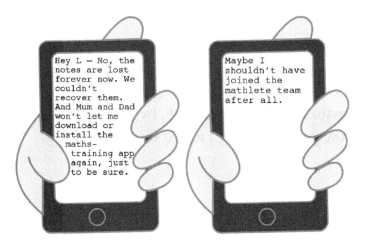

What?! Oh no, this called for some serious friend support and inspiration!

I waited at a table near the school library's entrance as the librarian, Mr Nile, paced carefully this way and that as he shelved some books, then pulled some more books off the shelves for another student. He was the typical picture of someone who likes to be with books all day, putting them in order and stuff. His short haircut was always super tidy and he always wore perfectly pressed slacks with shiny leather shoes and a button-down shirt done all the way to the top.

Tap ... tap. My foot wouldn't sit still as I waited. I hadn't heard back from Lucy after my last text, but I really hoped she would show up. She needed a spirit boost!

Finally, I saw Lucy come in and walk towards my table. Her shoulders were slumped, her feet dragged and it looked like her usually neat hair hadn't been brushed this morning. It was sticking up every which way.

"Hi," I said brightly as she sat down next to me and plopped down her backpack.

"Hey." She gave a weak smile. I kept my mood cheery as I slid an open notebook along with a pen over to the spot in front of her on the table.

"Here, you'll feel better once you see how much you remember. What was the first thing in your notes?" I prompted encouragingly.

Lucy let out a heavy sigh, but picked up the pen anyway. She thought for a moment then wrote something down – something about polygons and measuring the sides. My brain whirled from just looking at it!

In thirty minutes, Lucy had written down almost everything from the notes document she'd lost, plus some new stuff she'd learned in class today. And this copy wouldn't be lost since it was on actual paper – well, unless she misplaced it. She even beamed a smile at me once we'd finished!

"I guess it was all up here." She tapped the side of her head. "You and Kevin were right. Thanks, Elle, you're the best!" And she gave me a hug, then packed up her stuff.

"I better get going to meet the team over at the competition. It starts in one hour! I'll see you there – bye, Elle!" She waved and sped off.

"Bye, Lucy, see you at the competition soon! Good luck!" I called after her, maybe a little too loudly. I got a stern look from Mr Nile who liked voices kept to a whisper at all times in the library.

I didn't care though. My mission had been accomplished. Lucy was back in good spirits and believed in her own genius abilities again! Yay me!

I met up with Maya, Dennis, Lizzy and Tom after rushing out of the library, and we all took a bus over to the other school where the maths competition was being held.

Just before it started and we had to take our seats in the audience, I found Lucy standing with the two other team members. Wow, they looked sooo much older, and both towered over Lucy and me – eek!

The older boy had bright red hair and really did fidget a lot like Lucy had told me. He fixed his hair, shifted his glasses, adjusted the top button on his shirt and kept his feet shuffling back and forth. The girl just looked around with a knowing expression, her chin lifted to the air as if she was smarter than everyone. Which was sooo not true, of course. Lucy was way younger than her and just as clever!

"Hey, good luck, Lucy." I gave her a hug.

"Thanks, Elle, you're the best maths trainer – and friend – in the world!" She smiled at me.

Then it was time! I had to run and find a seat between Lizzy and Tom in the rows of metal chairs set up for the audience. I noticed Kevin and Lucy's parents sitting in the row ahead of us. I hoped Lucy and her brother had made up after that huge fight Wednesday.

I'd never been to anything like a maths competition before and found it was definitely different – but just as exciting – as a tennis match or the Twilight Run competition with Tom.

It was a large room with white walls and the audience faced a slightly raised platform at the front of the room where a podium stood in the centre. There were four teams competing from four different schools, including ours with Lucy, of course. Each team of three sat at long, rectangular desks – two desks on either side of the podium – and faced out.

Our school's team was on the left side and I could see little Lucy sitting in the middle with the older girl and boy on either side of her. She looked a bit pale and nervous, but happy.

Then, a woman walked to the podium and tapped on the microphone. A loud, teeth-grating high-pitched noise echoed through the room – screeeech – scriiitch! Eek! I covered my ears until the woman got the mic under control.

She welcomed everyone, introduced the teams and then it began. A large white screen at the front suddenly glowed with the first question along with a timer in the upper right corner to count down how much time the competitors had to finish the question.

The woman at the front called out, "On your marks, get set and … go!" She clicked something on her laptop, which made the timer on the big screen start to run down by the seconds.

"This is so exciting," Lizzy mouthed to me. I nodded and grinned.

The first question read: "The sales ad said: 'Buy three tyres at the regular price and get the fourth tyre for three dollars.' Jack paid two hundred and forty dollars for the set of four tyres at the sale. What was the regular price of one tyre?"

This one had already stumped me, but I watched Lucy up there, writing and tapping away on her calculator then consulting with her two team members as they worked it out.

Buzzzz-Beep! The question timer on the big screen sounded as it reached zero time left and all the teams had to say their final answers. The way it worked was that every time a team got the answer correct in the given time, they earned a certain number of points. If they ran out of time before getting an answer, it was zero points, and if they got the answer incorrect, they lost points.

But our team got the first answer right – yay! When the woman at the podium said Lucy's team's answer was correct, Lizzy, Dennis, Maya and I all clapped and cheered while Tom let out a "woo hoo, Lucy!"

But once we got a stern frown from the podium lady and harsh looks from some of the others in the audience, we all realised that maybe we should do silent cheering during the competition and save the loud stuff for the end. Whoops! How embarrassing!

So we watched and quietly applauded in our minds as they went through question after question.

Then our school's team made it to this final showdown between the top two teams at the end and did a 'rapid-fire' round with buzzers and everything! It got my blood pumping through my veins like crazy. Who knew maths could be so exhilarating?

In a very close final, our team ended up getting second place, which Lucy, the team and all of us were very happy about. We clapped and cheered when they handed out silver medals and Lucy held hers high above her head as we were finally allowed to whoop and holler and cheer nice and loudly!

The podium lady even said, "And the second-place team gets a very special award for having Lucy, the youngest member ever to be on a team at this level of maths competition!

Congratulations!" And the woman handed a rolled-up piece of paper with a red ribbon tied around directly to Lucy, whose face was bright pink and bursting with pride. Yay for our Lucy!

"You were amazing!" I told her afterwards when all of our friends and Lucy's family surrounded her with hugs and congratulations. Lucy pushed her glasses up on her small nose, turned pink and said, "It was super fun and we made second place as well as getting this special award! I couldn't have done it without your help, Elle. Thanks for practising with me, and boosting my spirits!"

Now it was my turn to blush. I waved a hand but gave a big smile. "It was easy, just asking questions. You're the maths whiz, Lucy!"

Everyone chimed in agreement, even Kevin who gave her a high five. It was good to see her and her brother back on good terms after that horrible argument!

Lucy's family invited all of us to walk to a café down the street for milkshakes and, of course, we all said yes and went for our cool, frothy treats. I had chocolate with whipped cream on top –

mmm-mmm. Sooo yummy my stomach did a happy dance as I drank it!

While it had been fun to help Lucy train – and fantastic that our team came in second place – I was happy to be getting back to my regular schedule, without quite so much maths. All those numbers and symbols and fractions were still swimming around in my head making me dizzy!

After the celebration, I was home and up in my bedroom, looking over all the notes I'd made in my diary during the week about what I'd learned from Lucy and her family's experience with the new tablet and computer.

- Always, always, always check with your parents or a trusted person before downloading and installing any new programs or apps onto a tablet or computer.

- Be super careful about personal information, photos and other stuff you put on the Internet since it stays there forever.

- Be aware of phishing (nothing to do with fishing and fish!) for personal information. Nasty people sometimes pretend to be someone they're not or send you scam emails to get your information.

- Never, ever click on links you don't know or emails from people you don't know.

- Don't share your password with anyone other than your parents or someone you trust.

- Always remember to log off when you're not using the computer or tablet, and don't snoop around other people's stuff.

- Always save your work (as you go) and make sure to back it all up just in case something happens, like a computer crash.

- Have a trusted person install a filtering program to block unwanted or icky content.

- It's very, very, very important to balance the time you spend on the tablet or computer with doing other things, especially stuff like physical activities and exercise. Too much time staring at a screen can hurt your eyesight or make it hard to sleep at night.

- Treat your computer or tablet with respect – don't get crumbs in the computer keyboard (eek), don't spill anything on it, keep it dry, put it in a case or bag to keep it safe and sound.

- Do all you can to avoid getting a virus (of the computer type, as well as the stuffy-nosed type).

- If you get a virus on your tablet or computer then get a parent or trusted person to help you fix it.

- And, there is a big, big, big difference between using a device, like your tablet, on your own home network and an external network. The cost is much, much higher when you're not using Wi-Fi, especially if you're overseas!

I had gathered so much cyber-safety information and learned so much from Lucy and her family's situation with the tablet and computer.

I am not perfect but I think I'm pretty close to it, and I'm always willing to learn!

And my final very important tip to remember:

Always tell a trusted adult straight away if something weird happens on the computer or something makes you feel uncomfortable.

Dear friends

Although a diary is private, I'm happy to share mine with you. I hope you enjoyed learning from my cyber-adventure.

Watch out for my next book. I'm sure it will rock your socks off and be another exciting cyber-journey.

Until next time, be safe when using and playing with technology.

Thanks for reading.

L

P.S. Thank you very much for reading my book! I hope you liked it.

I know your time is valuable. However, please take a brief moment to leave a review and I will appreciate it.

Your effort will assist new readers find my work, decide if the book is for them and help me with my future writing.

Thank you again, and be sure to keep a look out for the next book in my Diary of Elle series!

P.P.S. Want to find out more about me and my friends, please visit my website www.diaryofelle.com.

About the Series

The series, Diary of Elle, informs and inspires children's awareness of cyber-safety through fun stories in diary-format. Starring Elle (the diary-owner) and her friends, each book in the series of seven books will allow children to learn about a different cyber-safety concept through the experiences of other children.

About the Author

Nina Du Thaler began working in the Information Technology (IT) industry long before authoring her first book. She is also a mother of a 9 year old daughter (almost double digits!) and works as a Chief Information Officer (CIO), responsible for the IT environment within a large company in Australia.

She has experienced first hand the positive and negative impacts that technology can have on children's daily lives. It is pervasive and they use it easily and without hesitation, but they are unaware of potential consequences and we have not equipped our children to have the skills to deal with these challenges.

In the series, Diary of Elle, she combines her knowledge and experience in IT and parenthood, into a unique combination of fun products (featuring Elle and her friends), so that children can learn from other children's experiences.

Nina and Elle wish you fun reading, with some learning on the side!

Copyright Notice

Lucy's family launches into the cyber-world!
by Nina Du Thaler

ISBN: 978-1-925300-05-5

First published April 2017 by Bright Zebra Pty
Ltd.

Cover and illustrations by Fanny Liem
Edited by Helena Newton.

Special thanks to Bob Beusekom and Natia Meyers
:-)

Made in the USA
Middletown, DE
17 March 2023

27007599R00040